The Little Girls' Dance Class

Illustrated by J.-L. Macias S.
Retold by J. Carruth

Karen and Katy are best friends. They do most things together.
Every week they go to their dance class. Karen is very busy
talking to another little friend. She is always the last to change.
Hurry, Karen! The class can't start without you! Katy is wearing
two butterfly bows in her red hair. She has brought her doll,
Anna, to the lesson. "Anna can dance with your doll," she tells
one of the dancers. "They are just about the same size so they
can be partners."

Karen is ready at last and the teacher, far away at the end of the big room, claps her hands. "Positions please!" she calls, as she puts on the record. All the pupils know what to do. They pirouette and wave their arms in time to the music. Even old Terry Tortoise does his very best to join in and prove that he can dance too!

No wonder everybody is so tired. The dance class has been hard work. Sally has brought lollypops for each of her friends. They are all delighted.

Soon all the dancers go out to the garden. This gives Mother Duck and her seven beautiful babies a chance to show how well they can swim. Katy lies flat on her tummy so that she can watch Terry Tortoise enjoying his lollypop. "He really deserves it," she thinks. "Dancing on four legs can't be easy!" Karen wonders if her doll would like a taste of her lollypop.

The sun shines down on all the little dancers. It is very quiet until a big dog appears. He sees the teacher's cat.

Suddenly, the peace and quiet of the pretty garden is over! The dog chases the cat around the pond, and Mother Duck takes to the air in alarm. That naughty dog is upsetting everything and everybody!

The cat finds a safe place at last. And
Karen and Katy want to make the
garden a happy, peaceful place again. Don't worry! Two of their
friends have a brilliant idea. They hurry away in search of the
dance teacher.

When they return, they have the
teacher's record player. Now the
garden is full of happy laughter again. The cat and the naughty
dog are the best of friends as they join in the fun. "It's the music
that is making everybody happy again," Katy whispers to her
doll, as she shows her the latest steps. "It really is the music!"

When it is time to go home, the dog and the cat say goodbye to each other just like old friends!

Published in the United States and simultaneously in Canada by Joshua Morris,
431 Post Road East, Westport, CT 06
Printed in Belg